et

ou discuss

this is a danc-

oaring

cloud

O my marvello

wants to roam with blazing trum

between drum-beats,

what is the reason ou smile, you smile?

the Thunderer,

nd your language wh

huddle feel so sweet sweet

tell wor

Jumbo hotdogs. Jumbo hamburgers. Jumbo

BLEAT BLEAT BLEAT

of once-upon-a-time and happily-ever-after

for it is said a b..k ...ur word

passed on is a p

arior's ring the thunder's rumble. you discuss

word will be love's bright blade

W of ainbow

Follow
that
Word

rtbeat heartbeat heartbeat.

isturb the peace. So what did

Not for nothing am I Th all verbs,

trumpet-blasts,
once-upon-a-time and happily-ever-after happenings.

Follow that Word

John Agard

Illustrated by
Momoko Abe

HODDER CHILDREN'S BOOKS

First published in Great Britain in 2022 by Hodder & Stoughton

5 7 9 10 8 6 4

Text copyright © John Agard, 2022
Illustrations copyright © Momoko Abe, 2022

The moral rights of the author and illustrator have been asserted.

A CIP catalogue record for this book
is available from the British Library.

ISBN 978 1 44496 497 4

Printed and bound in Great Britain by Clays Ltd, Elcograf S.p.A.

The paper and board used in this book
are made from wood from responsible sources.

MIX
Paper from
responsible sources
FSC® C104740

Hodder Children's Books
An imprint of
Hachette Children's Group
Part of Hodder & Stoughton Limited
Carmelite House
50 Victoria Embankment
London EC4Y 0DZ

An Hachette UK Company
www.hachette.co.uk

www.hachettechildrens.co.uk

To Anne McNeil
and her shepherding editorial eye
over the years

What is the hedgehog's prickly back
to come out now
of once-upon-a-time and happily-ever-after
How do you eat your words?

Contents

For without my telling pause

why broadcast it to the world

when kindness speaks for itself?

to surrender

Do words keep secrets?

Have you ever wondered why

Foreword

Do words keep secrets?

Have you ever wondered why a book of maps is
called Atlas after a Greek god?

Did you know a hurricane got its name from the
Carib god Huracan?

In this new collection John Agard, the first poet to
win the Booktrust Lifetime Award, takes you on
an exciting and thought-provoking journey into
the world of words. Here you'll meet eponyms,
inventive spins on Biblical sayings, characters from
history and mythology, not to mention calypso
poems that touch on serious matters with
a happy beat.

To Be Polite

To be polite to morning,
simply say good morning to you morning,
thank you for showing up on time as you do,
your sunray eyeball blinking in the blue.

To be polite to night,
simply say good night to you night, sleep tight,
bless you for your overhead duvet of stars
and for bringing the moon so close yet so far.

To be polite to dew,
simply say make yourself at home, dew,
let your silver linger in a vein of air,
turn a blade of green to a fleeting chandelier.

simply say good night to you night.

Mind, What Exactly Are You?

Mind, hope you don't mind,
but what exactly are you?

A mirror
where reflections gather?

A cupboard
where secrets harbour?

A window
where memories linger?

A doorway
where outside thoughts enter?

A wall

to keep out the stranger?

A bridge

that links other with other?

Mind, do you outlive flesh and bone?

Mind, have you a mind of your own?

Iris

The iris of the eye owes its name to the Greek goddess Iris, known for her robe of bright colours and trailing rainbow.

Wee rainbow
ribboned
in the cloud
of an eyelid's
flutter

a dance
of colour
gift-wrapped
in a glance
of atoms

a speck
of spectrum
in the tiniest
of circles
yet a cosmos

thanks be to Iris
for marvels
glimpsed
in a morsel
of light.

A Brief Encounter

I met this man with green skin and four eyes.
He told me he'd just migrated from the skies.

'Oh pity you poor short-sighted terrestrials.
You've been short-changed when it comes to
opticals.

I can close two of my eyes when I sleep at night
while my other two read by built-in satellite.

So now you know the very simple explanation
for our advanced extra-terrestrial civilisation.'

Sadly, he vanished, leaving me wondering
whether an optically challenged earthling

and a green person of super multi-tasking vision
could ever find what's called common ground?

Who knows, despite my thick-framed spectacles,
there's a chance we might have been compatible.

Mirror Mirror

I am the mirror on the wall.
Dare to look into my telling glass.
I speak the truth to all who ask.

Like my distant cousins, Moon and Sun,
I too delight in revelation.
I will show your future to your past.

I reflect the You behind the mask.
Wipe from me the dust of your deeds. Try.
I have one fault. I cannot lie.

So come on, ask the burning question.
Break me, if my answer displeases.
I speak louder when I speak in pieces.

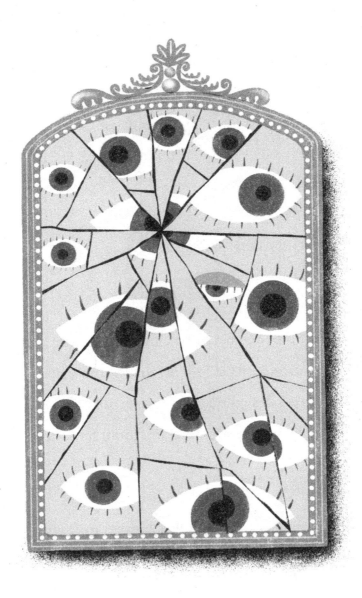

Two To Catch On (calypso poem)

It's been around from Creation dawn
and it only takes two to catch on.
Try it, people, and you will see
this is a dance that can set you free.
It's called the dance of diversity,
yes, the dance of diversity

See the birds, the beasts, the fish, the flowers,
how nature doesn't skimp on shades and colours.
Yes, nature's design makes room for all skin types,
making room for spots, making room for stripes

See how Moon presides in a house of night
while Sun in gold gown plays hostess to daylight.
And is so the lamb found joy in leaping
And is so the snake saw hope in creeping

See how Sky-bright keeping de day blessed

while Earth making dark ground a holy bed.

And is so Fire took pride in a flicker

And is so Water was pleased to trickle

It's been around from Creation dawn,

and it only takes two to catch on.

Try it people, and you'll soon see

this is a dance that can set you free.

It's called the dance of diversity,

yes, the dance of diversity

The Storyteller Of The Living Room

Once upon the long, long ago,
for ears gathered round fire's glow,
the storyteller would cast a spell
from the cauldron of a throat.

Now the storyteller talks by channel
and a control called remote.

Once upon a rock of cave for home,
the storyteller rattled skin and bone
and robed in words the ancient dead
gesturing darkness into legend.

Now the storyteller stares straight ahead
and applauds itself with canned laughter.

Yet heart still leaps at *happily-ever-after*

even for the tribe now squatting on a sofa.

The Giants' Lament For Beanstalk Jack

It should a' been our lucky day,

when a beanstalk brought him our way,

that Jack, yes, that titch of a lad,

might a' been the son we never had

How was we to know the lad's wits was sharp?

Done a runner with purse, with hen, with harp,

not to mention them beans nicked from our stalk.

How was we to know mortals can't be trusted,

but that's past now, all done and dusted

The scallywag seemed so sweet, so innocent,

we thought the poor creature heaven-sent.

At long last, the answer to our prayer,

some little someone for to stroke and care

A longed-for child for a family member,
we could a' frolicked o'er rock and heather,
that Jack could a' been our wee playmate,
our adopted one, but now too late, too late

How was we to know the lad's wits was sharp?
Done a runner with purse, with hen, with harp,
not to mention them beans nicked from our stalk.
How was we to know mortals can't be trusted,
but that's past now, all done and dusted.

Sir Lanceless To The Rescue

No doubt you've heard of Lancelot,
that brave Sir of Camelot –
home of King Arthur and his lot.
For the record, I'm Sir Lanceless.

If truth be told, I'm really not
the type cut out to be a knight.
Somehow a coat of shining armour
doesn't suit me. I don't feel right.

So how can a scaredy like me
rescue princesses from towers
when I'm allergic to heights
and stay well clear of elevators?

I, Sir Lanceless, would be useless

at saving damsels in distress

when slaying a poor dragon

is not exactly my idea of fun

And the thought of chopping briars

gives my skin hair-raising shivers.

As for riding a horse, forget it!

You won't catch yours truly near one.

I've come to the conclusion

that all things being considered,

my sword will be love's bright blade,

my shining armour my tongue.

On Alert

How lucky those armadillos
with their nine-banded defence.
The same goes, I suppose,
for skunks with their pre-emptive stench.

What is the hedgehog's prickly back
if not an arsenal of arrows?
And beware the porcupine's
on-alert infantry of spines.

As for that pangolin
it carries a castle in its skin.
And no smart-talking vertebrate
dare joust with a rhino's built-in breastplate.

Oh brainy humankind, whoever you be,

your skin seems short of weaponry.

What does it do for your morale

to be an un-armoured mammal?

Now You Know Why Peewit Sings The Blues

So, let the symphony begin.
Enter Blackbird, Skylark, Starling,
to announce the morning
alongside Crow's **caw-cawing!**

Now Cuckoo's **cuck-oooooo!**
reminds me that Spring is due.
And in the marshes that sound-cue
must come from the beak of Curlew.

And Willow Tit's **zee-zee-zee!**
sounds like a number one hit to me.
But these days when I scatter crumbs,
the chorus of birds remains dumb.

Now I know why. On the breaking news

I heard something called pollution's on the loose.

So now you know why Peewit sings the blues,

so now you know why Peewit sings the blues

Butterfly?

A butterfly perched on a butterfly bush
liked to ask her butterfly mum and dad
questions of the kind you'd call precocious:
'Might I ask why my name is butterfly,
when butter is the last thing I'll ever try?
In fact, stuck in butter, I'll surely die.'

To that question her parents had no answer.
All they could think of saying by way of reply
was: 'Now, aren't you a clever little butterfly?
Such awkward questions put us on the spot.
But count your blessings, butterfly child.
Give thanks you weren't named Nutterfly.'

And that kept her quiet. At least for a while.

And that kept her
quiet.

At least for a while.

Take A Bow, Swan

Ballerina
   of the lakes

   with a neck
like yours
   who needs toes
to pirouette?

And how well
   your tutu
of feathers
becomes you.

Take a bow, Swan.

Water your stage.

Every ripple

a swirling ovation.

Politically Correct Platypus
(calypso poem)

At first scientists thought we were a hoax.

The Creator having an almighty joke.

But calling us duck-billed isn't funny to us.

Maybe to Humans, but not to we Platypus.

That's no way to speak of what we like to call

our extra-sensory apparatus. No way at all.

Remember, you Humans,

Platypus too have Mammal status.

Mind your language when you discuss

our electro receptor, thank you very much

Though humans call us whatever they will,

we'll forgive them their duck as well as their bill.

Duck-billed, we say, is politically incorrect,

but we Platypus, we don't fuss and fret.

No, we maintain our pride, our reticence,

in the face of human impertinence.

Remember, you Humans,

Platypus too have Mammal status.

Mind your language when you discuss

our electro receptor, thank you very much.

The Decibels

Alexander Graham Bell (1847-1922) is
best-known for his invention of the telephone. He
worked with the hard of hearing. From his name we
get Bell, a unit for measuring noise levels. A decibel is
one tenth of a bell.

FOR GOD'S SAKE TURN THAT
    NOISE DOWN!
the disturbed residents would yell
to their neighbour from hell, Mr Decibel.

'You ain't heard nothing yet,' replied Mr Decibel.
'Wait till you hear my grandad, Mr Bell.
Trust me, the old boy's noises cast a spell.'

Then in moved senior Mr Bell,

ten times louder than his grandson, Decibel.

The neighbours turned to despairing.

'Forgive the disturbance,' apologised old Mr Bell.

'But I'm doing me best for the hard of hearing.'

Suddenly, this new neighbour from hell

became ear-splittingly endearing.

Sadly, when Messrs Decibel and Bell migrated,

the silence they'd left behind got overbearing.

Noise

I disturb the peace. So what if I do?
My name is Noise. I demand my due.
I give not a tut for your Hush!
or that precious finger to the lips.

Let a nation stand for a minute's silence.
Sixty seconds later, no more, no less,
I return to a city's throat replenished
to re-scatter my ear-splitting decibels

and turn all hearing to a living hell.
Yes, that's when I, **Noise**, assault the air
in the forms of sirens, a metallic fanfare
of pneumatic drills, a caterwauling din.

Without me, the world would be o-so bereft.

A world of silent self enduring silent self.

Silence

Thriving in the silent upsurge of seed,
I, Silence, tune in to the voiceless who bleed.

To the burdened ear I deliver welcome rest.
Lucky are those who count my presence blessed.
For without my telling pause between drum-beats,
trumpet-blasts, soaring strings, tapping feet,

is the ear not deaf to rhythms high and low?
So look for me in the shade of the crescendo.
Between the spaces, between the lines, I live.
Without me how hear that proverbial pin drop

in the calm before the shivers of a scary movie?
My void makes footsteps all the more creepy.
Yes, just when nerves tingle to silver screen terror,

my pregnant lull invites the monster to enter.

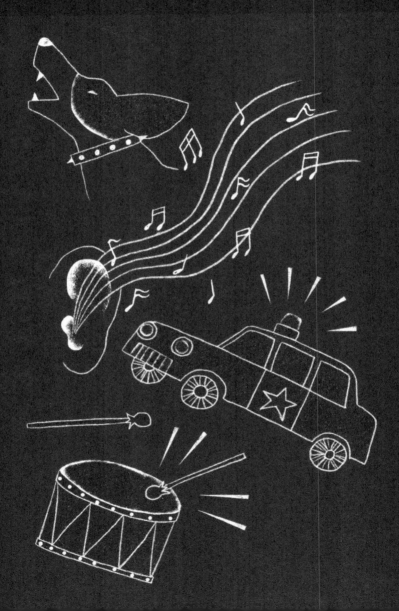

Thor's Day

Thursday got its name from Thor, the Norse thunder-god, while Friday (Frigg's Day) belongs to Frigg, goddess of fertility, and Saturday to the gloomy Roman god, Saturn.

My hammer's flash the lightning's crack.
My chariot's ring the thunder's rumble.

Not for nothing am I Thor, the Thunderer,
who makes the sky his resounding anvil.

But can't wait to see the back of Wednesday,
for come Thursday, Thor's day, I like to chill.

Time to unwind. Me-time! No giant to slay.
No storm-whipping, no mountain-bashing.

Not on Thor's day, thank you very much.

On Thor's day, let Thor's weekend begin.

A god's hammer deserves a mighty lie-in.

Memo to an Empty Diary

Dear diary

still fresh

as January,

stay blank

as blank can be.

Discover

the meaning

of days called free.

Dear diary

Dear diary

January, blank

free.

Atlas

In geography your book of maps got its name from
Atlas, the Greek Titan who tried to topple Zeus, the
Big Chief of the gods, and Atlas's punishment for this
was having to hold up the pillars of heaven.

Atlas, you may be giant and god rolled into one,
yet I pity those poor shoulders of yours
having to hold up the weight of the world.

Imagine, having to bear heaven's pillars
on your shoulders for all of eternity.
All I can say is better you than me!

How do you manage to keep calm and carry on?
If it had been my shoulders, I reckon
by now the sky would have had a tumble.

As you and the world together grow older,

my only prayer for you, Atlas,

is that you don't dislocate your shoulder.

But if holding up the world ever gets you down,

and you find yourself suffering from boredom,

well, there's always my weakling shoulders to lean on.

Ceres

To the Greeks she was Demeter. To the Romans
she was Ceres, the harvest goddess. Her name
is associated with wheat and lives on in
breakfast cereal.

Respect to you Ceres,
protector of crops.
Perhaps you'd fancy
a bowl of cocoa pops?
Or will a corn goddess
be even more impressed
by these crunchy nut flakes?
O Ceres, may you be pleased
with my cereal intake.

a bowl of cocoa pops
corn goddess

Melba Toast

Born Helen Porter Mitchell (1861–1931), the famous
soprano from Melbourne was known as Nellie Melba.
The story goes that while staying at the Ritz Hotel on
a tour of London, she insisted that French chef, Georges
Auguste Escoffer, do her toast not quite burnt, but
pretty close. Melba toast is named after her.

In heaven's super-deluxe diner
where they serve organic ambrosia
sits Dame Melba, a prima donna ghost.
The soprano at home in wings and halo
but none too pleased with her slices of toast.

'Waiter, I'm outraged!' she declares.
'Go tell the chef this toast is ill-prepared.
Well-burnt brown means well-burnt brown.

By thinly sliced I mean thinly sliced.
Don't let me have to say this twice.'

And there and then the celestial Chef
bellows from clouds of culinary mist:
'Dame Melba, this is not the Savoy or the Ritz.'

Jumbo

The first African elephant to arrive at London Zoo
arrived from Paris on 26 June 1865 and was given the
name Jumbo. It weighed over a massive six tons!

Jumbo hotdogs. Jumbo hamburgers. Jumbo jets.
And still Jumbo the elephant isn't impressed.
No, Jumbo's ghost just wants to forget
all those caged zoo days and circus bands.
Just wants to roam with blazing trumpet
across open spaces once called homelands.

Jumbo hotdogs. Jumbo hamburgers. Jumbo
Jumbo hotdogs. Jumbo hamburgers. Jumbo
Jumbo hamburgers. Jumbo
Jumbo hotdogs. Jumbo hamburg

The Last Shall Be First And The First Shall Be Last?

If this were true

how come

it doesn't work

in a queue?

Is someone

having a laugh?

'Well,' said Grandma,

'the last shall be first

and the first shall be last

is the back road to wisdom.

Mark my words for ever after.
There's a time and season

for the pudding to come
before the starter.'

Bleat Bleat Bleat (calypso poem)

BLEAT BLEAT BLEAT

we like to repeat,

we-Sheep find repetition

sweet sweet sweet

like heartbeat heartbeat heartbeat

We-Sheep don't make a fuss

when humans choose the likes of us

for their Sunday main course.

No, you won't hear Sheep whine

when roast lamb is de next in line.

See you there browsing de menu,

Sheep on a plate, can't argue

BLEAT BLEAT BLEAT

we like to repeat

we-Sheep find repetition

sweet sweet sweet

like heartbeat heartbeat heartbeat

Meanwhile, at night who counting Sheep

in their busy countdown to sleep?

Not Sheep, not Sheep, no not Sheep.

Humans think Sheep ain't clever,

how Sheep does blindly follow Sheep,

but what wrong with huddling together

like one big happy peaceful family?

Something Humans can learn from we.

BLEAT BLEAT BLEAT

while you huddle together

the more the merrier

the woollier the better

huddle feel so sweet sweet sweet

like heartbeat heartbeat heartbeat.

If It Ain't Broke, Why Fix It?

In a place known as *Back Of Beyond*
the locals were happy to carry on
living their days according to their gods
and the good will of the seasons.

Every morning they would sit in a circle
facing east to greet the rising sun,
all the while bowing to the ground
as they chanted *'If it ain't broke, why fix it?'*

Every night they would dance in a ring
bringing their gods flowers, fruit, carvings,
and blowing kisses to the moon and stars
as they chanted *'If it ain't broke, why fix it?'*

One day a stranger dressed in lilywhite
from an elsewhere place called overseas
(a spectacled over-qualified expert
in anthropological studies)

said: 'Tell me what good are your prayers
when your words fall on ears of stone?
What's the use offering flowers and fruit
to gods who are deaf as well as mute?'

The Back Of Beyonders gave a pitying sigh
and pointed to the four directions.
'Stones are the earlobes of the gods,'
they cried. *'So better mind your tongue.'*

Suddenly the stranger found himself transfixed.

Yes, rooted to the one spot as if in a trance.

Not wanting to upset his hosts or take any chance,

the expert joined in with *'If it ain't broke, why fix it?'*

t ain't broke, why fix it?'

'If it ain't broke, why fix it?'

'If it ain't broke, why fix it?'

Final Warning

Tell words
to lay down
their weapons

tell words
to surrender
all verbs, nouns,

adjectives, whatever
they have concealed
up their double-meaning sleeves.

Tell words
they're surrounded
by guns

tell words

to come out now

with their syllables in the air

or we'll be forced to declare

a public

curfew against the tongue

and cannot be held responsible

for the sudden

disappearance of all babble.

A Bag Of Gold And A Bag Of Books

There are these two men travelling in a canoe.

Each has a bag of books and a bag of gold.

Alas! Feels like the canoe is sinking. What to do?

They have a choice – to drown or lighten their load.

In the end they both agree to get rid of two bags.

The question – which bags do they throw overboard?

One man decides to hang on to his bag of gold.

So he chucks his bag of books into the river.

The other man hangs on dearly to his bag of books

and dumps his bag of gold without a second thought.
Luckily, they cross to the other side in one piece.
Border guards then escort them to the Royal Palace.

In the presence of the King the first man says:
'This bag has travelled with me a long way, Sire.
But feel free to have what gold you require.'

The King laughs: 'What would I want with
    more gold?
My bed's golden as my throne. I have gold aplenty.
As the saying goes, does one carry sand to the sea?'

Bowing before the King, the second man says:
'I threw my bag of gold back there in the river, Sire.
This bag of books here is all I have for treasure.'

Seeing a book for the first time in his life, the King
stares wide-eyed, yet thinks it wise to keep
    his distance.
Even his bodyguard stands back, leaving nothing
    to chance.

The King, curious (yet shall we say a little nervous)
    says:
'Your bag contains what's known as books? Is that so?
Pray, tell me, these books of yours, are they friend or
    foe?'

And so the man begins reading the King a story
of once-upon-a-time and happily-ever-after
    happenings.
Eyes closed, the King listens to the tale unfolding.

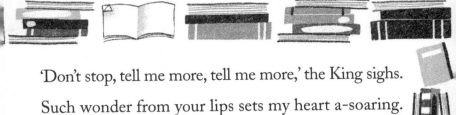

'Don't stop, tell me more, tell me more,' the King sighs.
Such wonder from your lips sets my heart a-soaring.
O let your telling fill my ears with enchanting lies.'

Then, offering the book to the King, the man says:
'A gift for Your Highness. You are welcome to
    the book,
for it is said a book passed on is a pleasure shared.'

The King clutches the book. Slowly lifts it to his ears.
His bodyguard coughs, doing his best to be polite.
'With due respect, Sire, you can neither read nor
    write.'

The King smiles: 'I have other plans for this book.
I think I've just found the cure for my nightmares.
This book for my pillow will make light my royal
    fears.'

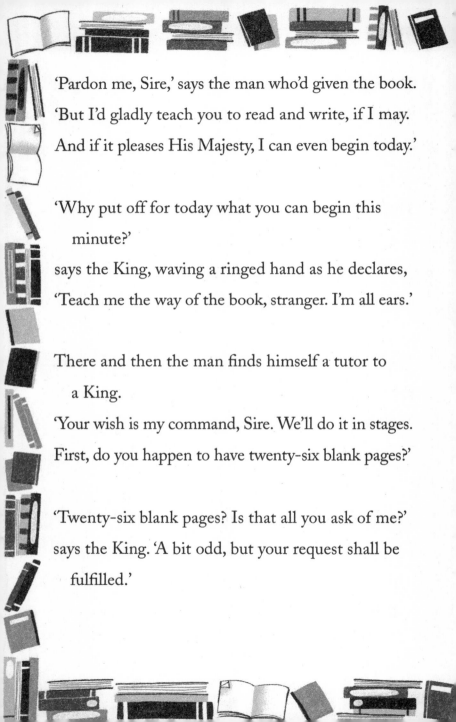

'Pardon me, Sire,' says the man who'd given the book.
'But I'd gladly teach you to read and write, if I may.
And if it pleases His Majesty, I can even begin today.'

'Why put off for today what you can begin this
      minute?'
says the King, waving a ringed hand as he declares,
'Teach me the way of the book, stranger. I'm all ears.'

There and then the man finds himself a tutor to
      a King.
'Your wish is my command, Sire. We'll do it in stages.
First, do you happen to have twenty-six blank pages?'

'Twenty-six blank pages? Is that all you ask of me?'
says the King. 'A bit odd, but your request shall be
      fulfilled.'

'If it's no trouble, Your Majesty, may I also have a
    quill?'

adds the man in his most courteous voice. The King
    says:
'Paper and quill shall be yours. And immediately!
I have no shortage of what's known as stationery.'

Then the King proudly displays a cabinet of glass
where stand stacks of paper inlaid with gold-leaf,
ancient quills and modern pens that staggered belief,

not to mention ivory inkwells all the way from China.
The man thinks to himself, *Oh what an impressive sight
for someone like this King who can neither read nor write.*

Sensing the man's surprise, the King goes on
    to explain:

'All gifts from ambassadors of the East and the West.
Designer pens, I'm told. But useless to me, I
    must confess.'

But in the twinkle of a flourish, the man inscribes
on separate blank pages the letters of the alphabet.
All twenty-six of them. Yes, the complete set.

Then, the man, pointing to the letters, one by one,
invites the King to imitate whatever sound
the letter stands for. So now the King rolls his tongue

around the plums of new-discovered vowels
    and nouns.
Ah, thinks the King. *I can get used to this alphabet.
And if it's the last thing I do, I intend to conquer it!*

As for this business of dotting i's and crossing t's,

a shame I left it so late. How these letters make me
  merry.
At this rate, I'll soon be called what's known as
  literary.

And so with time and patience on his tutor's part
(for the King, if truth be told, was a slow learner)
the King now reads and writes (even memorises
  by heart.)

To the end of his days, the King's head would be in
  a book.
But that book his tutor had given him on the day
  they met
would always serve him as his pillow for a sound
  night's rest.

Ottoman

The word ottoman comes to the UK from France, and prior to that from the Ottoman empire.

Othman, the first Turkish sultan,
rested his dreaming feet on an ottoman
as only an Ottoman sultan can.
So what if Othman the Ottoman
did not actually invent the ottoman?
I guess it makes one feel otterly grand
to have an ottoman for a faithful footstool
to serenely cushion your feet as you rule.

Now, centuries later, an ottoman
has come to mean a backless couch,
on which a couch potato can slouch
as only a modern couch potato can.

Will the likes of Othman the Ottoman approve

of a flat-packed self-assembled ottoman?

I guess not, for even in the Ottoman Empire,

there wasn't what's known as a Phillips screwdriver.

Passing The Buck

Don't blame me, said the gun.
Wasn't me that pulled the trigger.
Don't blame me, said the bullet.
Wasn't me that chose the target.

Don't blame me, said the landmine.
All I did was lie under the earth.
Don't blame me, said the shrapnel.
How was I to know all flesh burnt?

Don't blame me, said the soldier.
All I did was follow orders.
They told me to shoot on sight
whatever moves across borders.

Blame me, said the table, on my wood

were those deadly papers signed.

No, say my ink spilled a nation's blood,

blame me, cried one little pen.

What say you, medalled gentlemen?

And to that they all cried *Amen!*

Hercules Senior And Hercules Junior

1

Come to think of it, he was super strong for

  a toddler

(curling dumbells in his pushchair.) Like his dad,

  sturdy as rock,

yet Hercules Junior, a shy boy, seemed a bit shocked

by some of the photos in the family album. Like
   the one
taken after his dad had just killed the Nemean lion.
In lion skin coat, there stood Hercules Senior
   grinning.

But Hercules Junior couldn't help feeling sorry for
   the lion.
Not fair, he thought. Who would want to cause pain
to His Royal Highness Of The Golden Mane?

And there's another photo of his biceps-bulging dad,
this time standing over a weeping nine-headed
monster.
That snapshot always made Hercules Junior
feel sad.

Of course, Hercules Senior loved nothing better
than thumbing through photos from his legendary
past.
'What's that wild pig called again?' Hercules Junior
asked.

'That's the Erymanthian Boar. No match for the likes of me!'

Hercules Senior replied proudly with the wink of an eye.

'On that day, my boy, the crowds lifted me shoulder-high.'

To tell the truth, Hercules Junior was already a bit bored

of all his dad's back-tracking down memory lane.

Telling the same old stories again and again and again.

But he'd smile politely. 'Dad, I've heard that one

many a time.

Never mind. But didn't you also kill some

Ceryanaean Hind?

Or was it – let me guess – the Stympalian birds?'

2

But Hercules Senior was never one to take a hint.

So he'd reach for the kitchen mop and hop on to
the table,

pretending he was cleaning up some royal mucky
stable.

No, there was no stopping Hercules Senior in
full flow.

'Son, these photos take me back a long long way

to a time when I was an A-list celeb. A famous hero!'

His dad sighed: 'The old memory ain't what it used
to be.
But remind me, son, did I or did I not mention
the cattle belonging to the three-bellied giant, Gyron?

Forgive me if I did, but the tale is worth repeating.
Some, would you believe it, dared accuse me of
cheating.
The cheek of it! And all because I'd got a helping
hand

from your granddad, mighty Zeus. Chief god who
   ruled all.
Cheating indeed! It wasn't like I'd tampered with a
   cricket ball.
Anyway, to cut to the chase, as they say in the movies,

I managed to sail to the most western end of the
   earth.
Along the way I had to split a mountain that
   blocked my path.
But nothing was going to stop me accomplishing
   my mission –

which was to capture and bring back the red oxen
of Gyron.

That giant came after me, running on his three
pairs of legs.

So with my arrow I felled the triple-headed
monster. Job done!'

At this point Hercules Junior was doing his best not
to yawn.

These days his dad's fading memory would play tricks.

He'd get things all mixed up. Like calling his tenth
task his sixth.

'Hope I'm not boring you, boy, but oh how beautiful
it felt wrestling bare-handed with that Cretan bull.
He put up a good fight but couldn't handle my
    left hook.'

Hercules Junior was about to say, 'Enough, Dad,
    please!'
when Hercules Senior, pointed to another snap and
    said, 'Look,
son, there's Daddy saddling the horses of King
    Diamodes.

Well, those horses fed on human flesh, believe
   you me!
They weren't exactly what you would call veggie.
But with back-up from mates, I soon had the lot
muzzled.

Against all the odds, yours truly always came up
   trumps!
Yes, I outwitted every challenge, or if you prefer,
   every labour.
Back then I was a role model, a national
   treasure, whatever . . .'

Then, out of the blue, Hercules Junior, turned to
his dad.

'Am I allowed to have a three-headed puppy for a pet?
I can call it Cereberus after that dog guarding
Hell's gate.'

And that would be the first time he'd ever see his
dad cry.

'From time to time, son, I get this feeling of deep
regret

when I remember how I roughed up that poor
creature.'

That night little Hercules, though mega-muscled
    like his dad,
went to bed thinking gentle thoughts of monstrous
    beasts,
thinking that every living thing has the right
    to breathe.

this feeling of deep regret

gentle thoughts of monstrous beasts,

every living thing

has the right to breathe.

Wave Of Hand

Funny, how a simple wave of hand
can mean different strokes
for different folks

From a teacher a wave of hand
might mean calm down, class, in your place,
exams staring you in the face.

From a preacher a wave of hand
might mean beware hell's fire and brimstone,
repent sinner, or be damned.

From a driving instructor a wave of hand
might mean remember the highway code,
a pedestrianised street is no-go.

From a diva a wave of hand
might mean love you loads as she blows
celeb kisses to all the fans.

From a conductor a wave of hand
might mean time to change the tempo
from very fast to very slow.

But from a dictator a wave of hand
might mean neither a *yes* nor a *no*,
a dictator's wave can leave you in limbo

so watch out when a dictator
(with or without dark glasses)
starts waving a hand to adoring masses.

Let Not The Right Hand Know What The Left Is Doing

When you do a good turn

why broadcast it to the world

when kindness speaks for itself?

Why not let your kind deed

be as silent as a seed

growing in the darkness?

As for telling my right hand

what my left hand is doing,

I'll confide in neither.

For hands have telltale fingers

that can speak like a mouth.

Soon your secret will be out.

No, I tell my secrets to my feet,

for feet are more discreet.

Feet keep secrets well-locked.

Who can a pair of feet

spill the beans to except

a pair of smelly socks?

Friction

Without friction,
I couldn't pluck a sound
from my guitar string.

Without friction,
on paper my pencil would slip,
on ice my shoes wouldn't grip.

Thanks to friction
the brakes on my bike work,
so I don't go flying.

But then there's that other friction
that creates shattered bodies
the sounds of dying.

I think these thoughts, sitting alone,

lost in my own friction,

rubbing hand on hand, stone on stone.

Lady Mosquito Blesses Her Babies

O my marvellous brood of commas
on a wriggling page of water

O my little pride-of-eye buds
my limb-light bundles of night joy

Go forth my six-legged cherubs
Go forth in a flutter of the dark

May your fleet of time be blessed with blood
And may the ears you storm number millions.

Mr And Mrs Rat's Lullaby To Their Newborn

Sleep baby Rattus,

sleep your beauty sleep

as any Rattus must.

Sleep tight baby Rattus.

Catch a nap by day

catch a nap by night

make the most, newborn,

of darkness and light

Whichever way, O little ones,

a rat is never a loser,

we Rats are crepus-cu-lar.

Got that? What can be cooler

than being crepus-cu-lar?
That means, little Rattus,
you'll grow up busy come dusk
and just as spot-on come dawn.

Now sleep, our cutey newborn,
sleep your beauty sleep.
May you in your sweet dreams
nibble slices of moon-cheese.

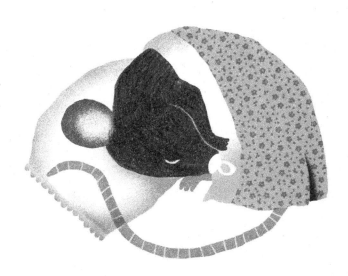

Juggernaut

Jagannath (an incarnation of the Hindu god Vishnu)
is celebrated at the festival of Rath Yatra with gigantic
wooden chariots being drawn through the streets
by Hindu and Buddhist devotees. Of Sanskrit
origin, meaning 'lord of the universe.' the British
mispronounced the word Jagannath as 'juggernaut' to
refer to a lorry.

Remember this, juggernaut,
you beast of a lorry
flaunting your bulk in a matter of tons

Remember this, I, Jagannath,
lord of the revolving universe,
deal only in measureless aeons.

Thunder my horsepower,

the moon my gear-changer,

the skies my eternal right-of-way.

O you poor traffic-jammed creature,

look on my chariot of sapphire

fuelled by no less than the cosmic air

then exhale your diesel and despair.

Eating My Words

How do you eat
your words?

With knife and fork
or with a spoon?

Are words sweet as a prune
or sour as a lemon?

One day I thought I'd eat
my words of venom

spat out in a moment's spite.
Those cruel words of mine

that now come back to haunt
my restless sleep at night.

But after I'd eaten those very words,
the feeling felt – well – sort of nice.

Now, I think before I speak,
Sometimes I even think twice.

Pomegranate?

I've just been told the word *grenade* (wait for it)
comes from the French for *pomegranate*

that fruit that detonates its nectar on the tongue
that fruit that inspired King Solomon's crown

that fruit whose mythic seeds anchored Persephone
to the Underworld for a third of the turning seasons

that fruit whose red juices still flow sweetly
through the veins of Persian poetry

that fruit whose skin is a blushing mirror
in which a bride may glimpse her ready threshold

that fruit whose bulbous self holds forth

a promise of abundance in the days to come

a far cry from that other fruit of similar shape

yet promising only bitter slices of oblivion.

Smart Bombs

A smart bomb has laser-sharp intelligence?
Did you say, gentlemen, a smart bomb is no dunce?

They laughed at Fool's ignorance
and spoke with great conviction.

'A smart bomb can outshine
the braincells of Einstein
for mathematical precision.
And as for long-range vision,
a smart bomb is almost divine.'

Again they laughed at Fool's ignorance
and said smart bombs leave nothing to chance.

'Gentlemen,' said Fool. 'One last question.

Do smart bombs count bodies laid limbless flat?'

'No, Fool, smart bombs are much too clever

for that.'

Huracan

*Huracan, the storm god of Mayan mythology, is also
the storm-god of the Carib Indians from whom we get
the words Caribbean, hammock (from hamaca) and, of
course, hurricane.*

You Huracan of the one serpent-leg
You whose breath can un-peg
the most stubborn of roots.
You whose embrace can reduce
a roof of stone to flying rubble.
You Huracan, thunder-heart of sky,
O lean your ear to the troubles
of the suddenly homeless
who pray with one question: *Why?*

You Huracan
of the one serpent-leg
You whose breath can un-peg

Poinsettia

*This flower had been used centuries ago by the Aztecs
as a dye and a cure for fevers. But the popular name,
Poinsettia, goes back to a certain Mr Poinsett, the
American Ambassador to Mexico in the late 1820s.*

Cuetlaxochitl
to Aztec ears.
Moctezuma's
favourite flower.
The star-shaped gift
that makes winter blush
and rewards the warrior.
Holy blood-bloom
that now bears
a diplomat's name.
Cuetlaxochitl

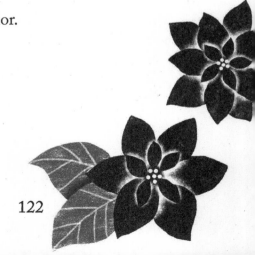

to Aztec ears.

Red as the tears

on a branch of memory

where the gods have left

the petals of their thumb-prints.

Quixotic

Don Quixote and his sidekick, Sancho Pancha, were two legendary characters from the Spanish novel **Don Quixote.**

Who comes riding so knightly out of the blue?
It is I, Don Quixote of La Mancha to you.
And I swear by the blood a good knight bleeds,
I ride no barnyard nag but a handsome steed.

To you my helmet may seem a barber's basin.
But do I look like a man who's lost his reason?
My shield may be old, and so is my lance,
but I am armed to the teeth in romance.

As for those giants with arms revolving to kill?
Well, only the foolish would call them windmills.

Those mega-monsters I shall fell with one blow.

Here comes I, Don Quixote, your quaint hero.

Newton's Apple

Sir Isaac Newton, the English physicist and mathematician, was hit on the head by a fallen apple while sitting under his apple tree in the summer of 1666. This led him to ask the question why do things fall towards the earth?

'This is the apple that fell
on Newton's head – the apple
that proved the law of gravity,'

said the auctioneer gravely.
waving his hammer in the air
with professional flair.

'This apple here made history,'
the auctioneer went on.

'After the head of Newton

this apple found itself
preserved for posterity.
So spare a thought for gravity.'

From the audience, Fool asks:
'Is the apple a cooking apple
or an eating apple? Please be clear.

Is that apple, say, a Bramley?
A Golden Delicious? A Pink Lady?'
The auctioneer gave a frown:

'Trust me, folks, all that matters
is that this apple fell on Newton.
And today it's under the hammer.'

'That may be so,' said Fool.

'But I never cook an eating apple,

nor do I eat a cooking apple.'

'My final question,' added Fool,

resorting to a what if and a but.

'But what if it had been a coconut?'

IF And BUT

IF holds the key
to what might
or might not be.

But when **BUT**
comes to mind
I pause a while.

IF opens the door
to what **IF**
imaginings.

IF points to
the path of endless
possibilities.

Then **BUT** steps in

to stop me

in my tracks

and take me back

to the beginning.

I must think again.

To **IF** and **BUT**

is there no ending?

But without **IF**

and of course **BUT**

you could find

yourself in a rut.

Thank you **IF**.

Thank you **BUT**.

Without you, I'm stuck.

holds the key

But when BUT

Thank you IF.

Thank you BUT.

Without you, I'm stuck.

Coffin

Carpenter Matthew Coffin (1480–1540) invented the wooden coffin box.

In your wooden box, Mr Coffin, you laid.
A humble carpenter by trade.
And far be it from me to be scoffing
at what the dead come softly in
(or should that be go softly in?)

But that ghost of yours, Mr Coffin,
to heaven's bank must be laughing,
for you will agree, Mr Coffin,
since the Grim Reaper comes often,
coffins keep the coffers coughing.

The Very Hairs On Your Head Are Numbered

If the very hairs on my head are numbered,
does that mean every single strand
of every single head in the world
has been counted by some invisible hand?

Then what about the scales on fishes,
the stripes on tigers, the feathers on birds,
the fur on rabbits, the spots on leopards?
I guess I'd better stop there.

But if all of these are carefully numbered,
how does God ever find time for slumber?
I can only conclude that the Creator
must be clever at maths. A cosmic calculator.

how does God ever find time for thinking?

In My Father's House There Are Many Mansions

What if I told you

that in my dad's house

there were many mansions

and that my mum's house

was blessed with just as many mansions?

What if I told you

that in my granddad's house

there were many mansions

and my grandma's house

was blessed with just as many mansions?

No, we're not rolling in money.

It's just that in our poor family

a rich heart is a house of many mansions

where the rooms are furnished with hugs

and the doors are made of welcome.

Three Seeds

A sad-faced gardener said to three little seeds:
'The choice is yours, I'll plant you wherever
  you please.
Now take your time, there's no hurry.'

The first seed said: 'To tell the truth, I'm not fussy.
As long as my roots get rain and sun, I'm easy.
Wherever I lay my roots, even stony ground, I'll
  call home.'

'Very well,' said the sad-faced gardener.
I'll plant you on stony ground if that makes you
  pleased.
And I think I'll call you by the name of Weed.'

The second seed said: 'Parchy ground is fine by me.

Parchy ground will do me for chilling out.

Watch this space! A bed of brambles I soon will

   sprout.

'Well, then, so be it,' said the sad-faced gardener.

'Have it you way. And since you've settled

for parchy ground, I think I'll call you Stinging

   Nettle.'

The third seed said: 'Good ground, thank you

   very much.

Nothing but organic compost will do for me

By that I mean ground rich in friendly fungi.'

The sad-faced gardener couldn't help smiling:
'Since you made me smile, and since you're
    so cheeky,
good ground shall be yours. And I'll call you
    Strawberry.'

Sadly, Strawberry got nibbled up by snails and slugs,
while Weed and Nettle thrived in the not-so-good
    ground.
This, of course, made the gardener's smile turn to
    a frown.

The Mermaid Turns to Plan B

Mermaid Mermaid, Mistress of the deep,
what is the reason you weep, you weep?

Because my comb, my precious ivory,
with which my ebony hair I did groom
by the light of the mirroring moon,
has been found and kept (o woe is me)
by the stealing hand of some earthling being.
And finders for me are not keepers,
such finders make mermaids weepers.
Cursed be whoever makes my comb their property!

Mermaid, Mermaid Mistress of the deep,
what is the reason you smile, you smile?

Because I've turned my loss to gain.

Looks like my comb will not be seen again,

so now I have turned to my plan B.

Yes, I've shaved my head completely.

See my head now all bald, all smooth,

a head to match the dome of the moon!

Let earthling beings keep what's not theirs,

tonight I curse them with a smile. No tears.

Underwater One-To-One

Once upon a salty morning
a deep-sea diver was kidnapped
by a school of dolphins

but the dolphins meant him no harm.
In their underwater classroom
they treated him to free lessons

in the art of dolphin breathing
without need for an oxygen mask.
This was no easy task.

The dolphins taught him that whistling
took more than two fingers
to fill an ocean's corridor.

The dolphins even taught him how
to whistle his own name
and this gave him quite a thrill.

The man just couldn't wait
to show off his new skill.
as he flippered his arms like his teachers.

But O the sudden harpoon-gun
that one day pierced a whistling human
trying out his dolphin tongue.

The First Prayer

What was the first prayer
Humankind ever said?

Was it an appeal
to Ice to show mercy
to nomad feet in need of rest?

Or a heart-felt plea
to Sun to hold back its fire
that the harvest

may not wither
in the arms of drought?

What was the first prayer
Humankind ever said?

Maybe a thank-you
for the hoped-for blessing
of rain come bathe dry ground?

Was it out of a deep down
need for the un-born?
A chat with the long-gone dead?

Yes, what was the first prayer
Humankind ever said?

Maybe that very first prayer
wasn't even uttered
in the shape of a word.

What was the first prayer

Becau... turned my ...

...ver find time for slumber?

John Agard was born in Guyana and emigrated to Britain in 1977. He has worked as an actor and a performer with a jazz group and spent several years with the Commonwealth Institute, travelling all over Britain giving talks, performances and workshops. He has visited literally thousands of schools. His poem 'Half-Caste' is on the AQA English GCSE syllabus, and every year he tours the country performing with other top poets for GCSE students. He lives in Sussex and is married to Grace Nichols, herself a respected Caribbean poet. In 2021, he was awarded the BookTrust Lifetime Achievement Award.

Momoko Abe was born in Japan and has been drawing ever since she can remember. Aged 20, pursuing her passion for visual storytelling, she came to the UK to study filmmaking, and still works in the TV and film industry alongside her illustration work. Momoko is an AOI World Illustration Award Shortlist artist.

She lives in London.

what is the rea

eason you smile, you smile?

what if had been a coconut?

what is the reason

what is t reason you smile, you smile?